The Night Before THE 100th DAY OF SCHOOL

Grosset & Dunlap

To Tess—N.W.
To Macey and Mack—M.P.

GROSSET & DUNLAP
Published by the Penguin Group
Penguin Group (USA) Inc., 375 Hudson Street, New York, New York 10014, U.S.A.
Penguin Group (Canada), 10 Alcorn Avenue, Toronto, Ontario, Canada M4V 3B2
(a division of Pearson Penguin Canada Inc.)
Penguin Books Ltd, 80 Strand, London WC2R ORL, England
Penguin Ireland, 25 St Stephen's Green, Dublin 2, Ireland
(a division of Penguin Books Ltd)
Penguin Group (Australia), 250 Camberwell Road, Camberwell, Victoria 3124, Australia
(a division of Pearson Australia Group Pty Ltd)
Penguin Books India Pvt Ltd, 11 Community Centre, Panchsheel Park, New Delhi - 110 017, India
Penguin Group (NZ), Cnr Airborne and Rosedale Roads, Albany, Auckland 1310, New Zealand
(a division of Pearson New Zealand Ltd)
Penguin Books (South Africa) (Pty) Ltd,
24 Sturdee Avenue, Rosebank, Johannesburg 2196, South Africa

Penguin Books Ltd, Registered Offices: 80 Strand, London WC2R ORL, England

Text copyright © 2005 by Natasha Wing. Illustrations copyright © 2005 by Mindy Pierce. All rights reserved.
Published by Grosset & Dunlap, a division of Penguin Young Readers Group, 345 Hudson Street, New York,
New York 10014. GROSSET & DUNLAP and READING RAILROAD are trademarks of Penguin Group (USA) Inc.
Printed in the U.S.A.

Library of Congress Cataloging-in-Publication Data

Wing, Natasha.
The night before the 100th day of school / by Natasha Wing ; illustrated by Mindy Pierce.
p. cm.—(Reading railroad)
Summary: When a little boy finally decides what to bring to the celebration of the one hundredth day of
school, he has no idea what a surprise it will be for everyone.
ISBN 0-448-43923-9 (pbk.)
[1. Hundredth Day of School—Fiction. 2. Schools—Fiction. 3. Hundred (The number)—Fiction.
4. Ants as pets—Fiction. 5. Stories in rhyme.] I. Title: Night before the hundredth day of school.
II. Title: Night before the one hundredth day of school. III. Pierce, Mindy, ill. IV. Title.
V. Series: Reading railroad books.
PZ8.3.W7185Niy 2005
[E]–dc22
2005003425

7 9 10 8

What'll I bring into school?
I need something in a hurry.

Already most kids have thought of their stuff.

Flip has 100 photos of his new puppy, Fluff.

Paul says he's
bringing pencils.

Carter's got
his cars.

Jane has 100 jelly beans.

Samantha, 100 gold stars.

So I got out my dinosaurs,
put them all in a line.
When I counted them up,
there were only forty-nine.

I dumped out my piggy bank—
pennies, nickels, and dimes.
I counted them twice
and came up short both times.

When what with my wondering
eyes should I see?
"No one else will bring ants.
No one but me!"

That night while I nestled
all snug in my bed,
visions of ants, ants, and more ants
danced in my head.

The very next morning, the big day was here.
Hooray for the 100th day of the school year!
So away to the school bus I flew in a flash . . .

then hopped off on the sidewalk
and made a mad dash.

Our class was eyeing a huge cake—
it smelled oh-so-sweet.
"Share Time first," said Mr. Stein.
"Then after, we'll eat."

Mabel went first—
with 100 marbles in a can.

Shana showed her sugar cubes.

Then came the twins, Stan and Dan.

Jocasta had 100 names on her cast.

And all of a sudden, it was my turn. At last!

I walked to the table at the front of the room.

But I tripped on a marble
and landed—

ka-boom!

The lid, it popped open!
Ants came running out!
"Here's one! There's one!"
kids started to shout.

One by one, my ants marched
straight toward the snack table.

"They're going for the cake!"
shouted Michael and Mabel.

I headed them off with crumbs from my lunch.
"Go back to the farm," I told the whole bunch.

Sixty . . . seventy . . . eighty . . . I counted through ninety-nine.
Where was the last one?

"On me!" said Mr. Stein.

"Now that Share Time is over
and the last ant is in . . .

"It's time for our party.
Let the celebration begin.
Are you ready for cake?"

We all shouted, "Yes!"

Then we blew out the candles.
How many? Just guess.